fire • fish • five • flag • flashlight • flower • fly • foot • football • fork • frog • funnel • **G** • gas pump • gemstone • ghost • gingerbread cookie • giraffe • glass • glove • golf ball • golf clubs • grapes • grave • guitar • gum • **H** • hamburger • hammer • hanger • hat • Hawaiian dancer • hay • helicopter • hen • hippo • hoe • hole • horse • house • Hula-Hoop • hydrant • **I** • ice cream • ice cream cone • ice cube • ice skate • igloo • iguana • inch • infant • ink • insect • iron • islands • **J** • jack-in-the-box • jack of hearts • jacket • jam • jar • Jell-O • jelly beans • jet • jogger • juice • **K** • kangaroo • kayak • kayaker • ketchup • kettle • key • keyhole • king • kiss • kites • kiwi • Kleenex • knight • knob • knot • koala • **L** • ladder • ladle • lady • ladybug • lamp • lasso • laundry • leaf • leg • lemon • leopard • letter • life preserver • lifeguard • lighthouse • lipstick • list • lobster • lock • locomotive • log cabin • lollipop • **M** • macaroni • map • mask •

an excessive ALPHABET

Avalanches of As to Zillions of Zs

AN EXCESSIVE
Avalanches of As to

atheneum

A Caitlyn Dlouhy Book • **Atheneum Books for Young Readers**

ALPHABET
Zillions of Zs

written by Judi Barrett

illustrated by Ron Barrett

New York   London   Toronto   Sydney   New Delhi

A

ATHENEUM BOOKS FOR YOUNG READERS
An imprint of Simon & Schuster Children's Publishing Division
1230 Avenue of the Americas, New York, New York 10020
Text copyright © 2016 by Judi Barrett
Illustrations copyright © 2016 by Ron Barrett
All rights reserved, including the right of reproduction
in whole or in part in any form.
ATHENEUM BOOKS FOR YOUNG READERS is a registered
trademark of Simon & Schuster, Inc.
Atheneum logo is a trademark of Simon & Schuster, Inc.
For information about special discounts for bulk purchases,
please contact Simon & Schuster Special Sales at
1-866-506-1949 or business@simonandschuster.com.
The Simon & Schuster Speakers Bureau can bring authors
to your live event. For more information or to book an event,
contact the Simon & Schuster Speakers Bureau at
1-866-248-3049 or visit our website at
www.simonspeakers.com.
Jacket design by Lauren Rille; interior design by Ron Barrett
The text for this book was set in Gill Sans.
The illustrations for this book were rendered in pen and ink
and colored digitally and alphabetically.
Manufactured in China
0217 SCP
10 9 8 7 6 5 4 3 2
CIP data for this book is available from the Library of
Congress.
ISBN 978-1-4814-3986-2
ISBN 978-1-4814-3987-9 (eBook)

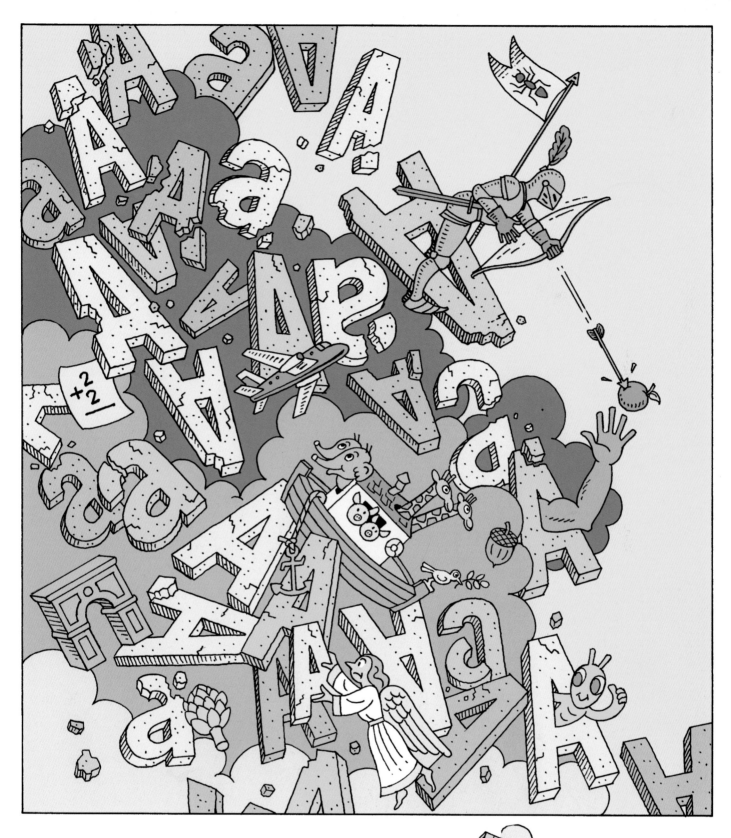

Avalanches of

Boatloads of B s

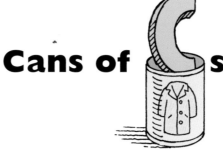

Cans of **s**

Dozens of  **s**

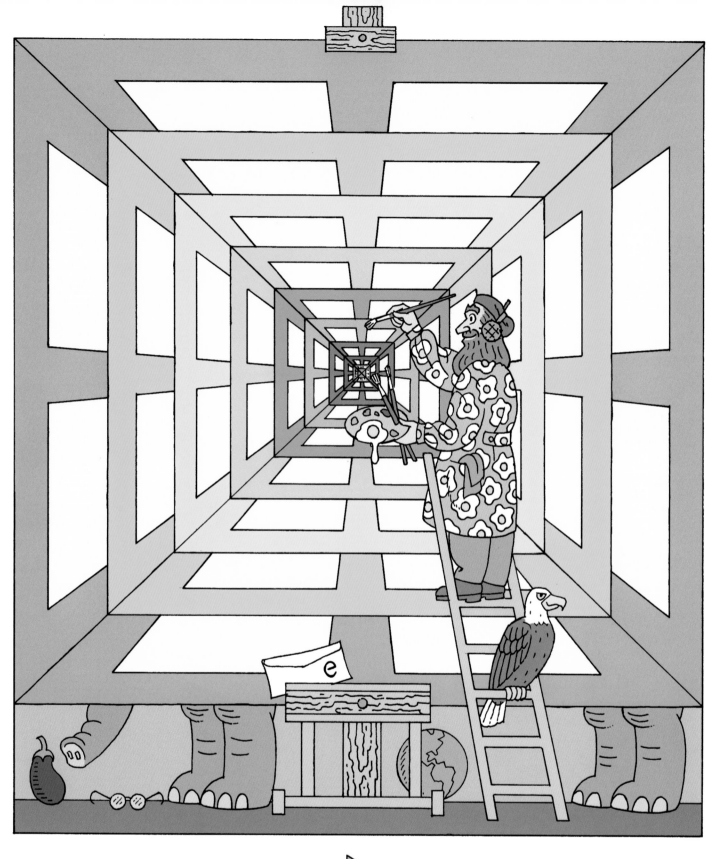

Endless E s

Flocks of **s**

Globs of  **s**

Herds of **s**

Islands of Is

Jumbles of J**s**

King-size s

Loads of 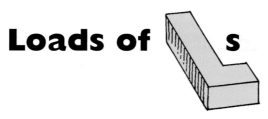s

Mountains of M s

Networks of s

Oodles of s

Piles of P s

Quarts of s

Racks of R s

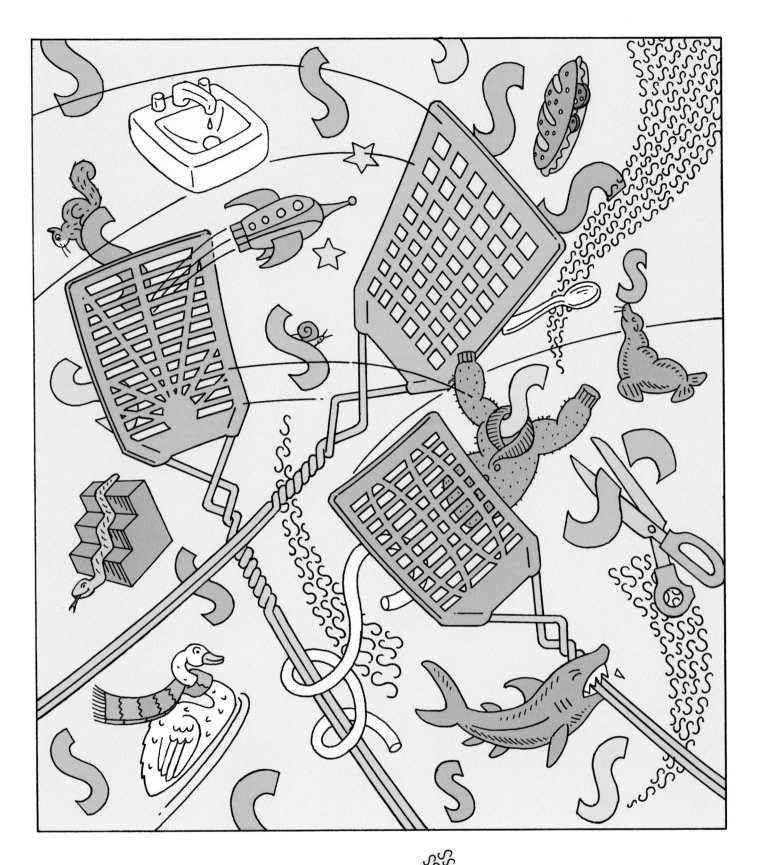

Swarms of S s

Truckloads of **s**

Umpteen  **s**

Volumes of 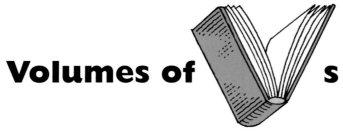 **s**

Whopping amounts of  **s**

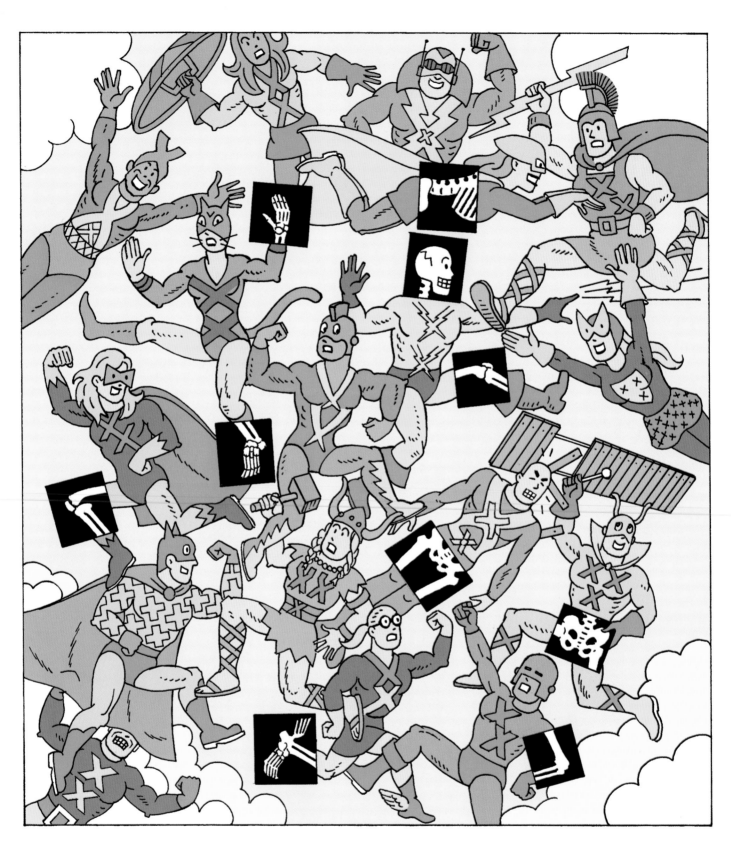

Xtra  **s**

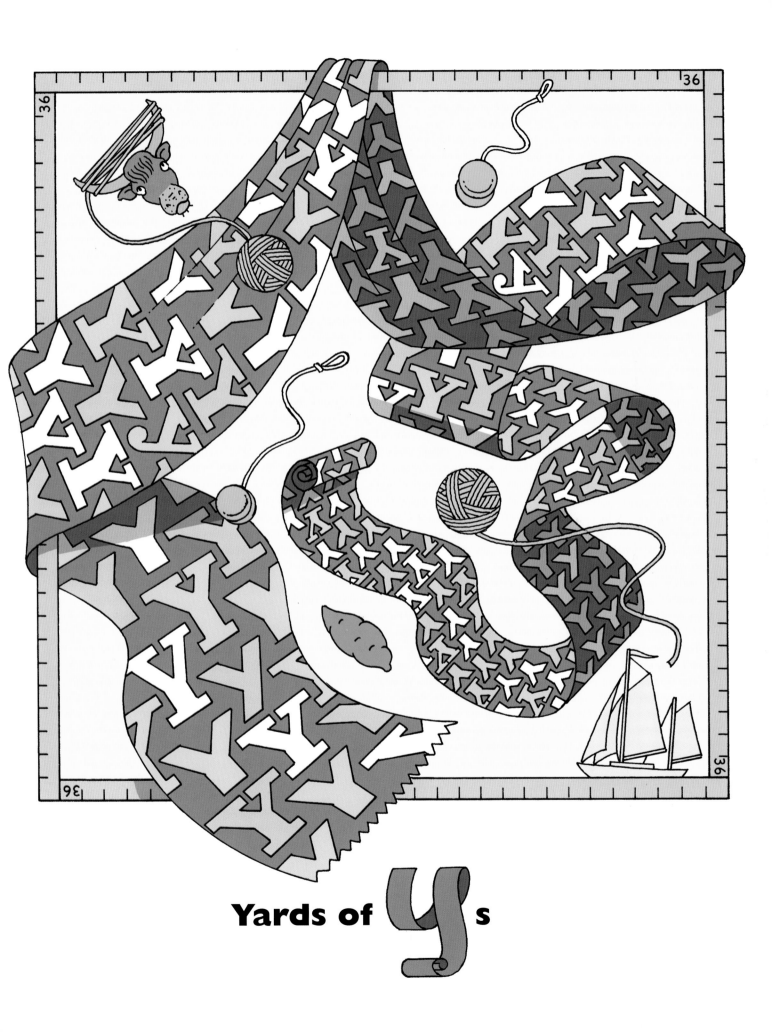

Yards of Y s

Zillions of  **s**

See how many of these things you can find in the pages of this book.

Here's a clue: if you know the letter of the alphabet the item starts with, look on that page . . . and you'll surely find it!

mayonnaise • medals • milk • mist • mittens • money • monkey • moon • mop • mountains • mouse • mug • mummy • mushrooms • mustache • mustard • **N** • nails • necklace • necktie • needle • nest • newspaper • nine • noodles • nose • note • nut • **O** • oar • octopus • oil • oil well • Olympic rings • one • opera • orange • Oscar statuette • ostrich • overalls • owl • **P** • package • paint • pancake • paper airplane • parachute • parrot • pear • peas • pen • penguin • pickle • pie • pig • pizza • plant • pot • pretzel • pumpkin • pyramid • **Q** • quack • quake • quarterback • quartet • quarts • queen • question mark • quill • quilt • quiver • quotation marks • **R** • raccoon • radio • radish • rag • rain cloud • rainbow • rattle • reptile • ribbon • rings • robe • robin • rock • roll • roof • rope • ruler • **S** • seal • scarf • scissors • shark • sink • snail • snake • spaceship